By Gerry and George Armstrong
THE MAGIC BAGPIPE
THE BOAT ON THE HILL

The Fairy Thorn

by GERRY & GEORGE ARMSTRONG

ALBERT WHITMAN & COMPANY · CHICAGO

Standard Book Number 8075-2241-4
©Copyright 1969 by Albert Whitman & Company
Library of Congress Card Number 75-79547
Published simultaneously in the Dominion of Canada
by George J. McLeod, Ltd., Toronto
Lithographed in U.S.A.

Ireland

Galway

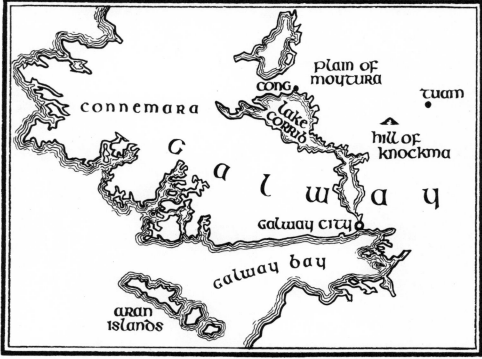

Plain of Moytura

Cong

Tuam

Connemara

Lake Corrib

hill of knockma

Galway

Galway City

Galway Bay

Aran Islands

AN OLD HAWTHORN tree—some people called it a fairy thorn—stood by a shining lake in the west of Ireland. Across a checkerboard of fields was a shepherd's cottage. And from the cottage came the sound of music and laughter. The O'Flahertys were having a party!

Mr. O'Flaherty played the flute, and Owen, his son, played the fiddle. It was a beautiful fiddle that had belonged to his grandfather. One of the guests played a bagpipe, another a drum.

The players chose jigs and reels and slow airs. How beautiful the Irish music sounded—it filled their hearts as well as their ears.

Later, when Mrs. O'Flaherty served tea and cake, Owen said, "Tell us a story, Father."

"Yes, do," begged his sisters, Mary and Meg.

"Well, now," said Mr. O'Flaherty, and the guests stopped chatting to listen, too. They all loved a good tale.

"Have I told you about the King of the Fairies?"

"Was he a leprechaun?" asked Mary.

"Ah, no," said her father. "A leprechaun is one of the little people, smaller than a real child. The other fairies are a grand size, big or bigger than we ordinary men. Your grandfather once met their king, Finvarra."

"Oh, tell us about that!" cried Meg.

"Well," said Mr. O'Flaherty, "long ago, and a long time it was . . ."

Just then there came a sharp knock on the door. Neighbor Burke stood scowling on the doorstep.

Mrs. O'Flaherty said politely, "Come in, Mr. Burke. You'll join us in a cup of tea, of course."

"No," the man snapped. "I've come to warn you, O'Flaherty. You must pay the money you owe me by May Day or the farm and the fiddle are mine."

Mr. O'Flaherty exclaimed, "But, Burke, surely you remember! You agreed to let me pay you after I sell the wool from my sheep. We shook hands on it."

Burke sneered, "Sure I have a bad memory. The paper you signed says May Day. I want my money by then—or else." And the door slammed behind him.

"How unfair! Burke is a moneygrubber and a cheat!" said the O'Flahertys' friends. But they couldn't help. None of them had any money.

"He can't take the fiddle and everything, can he, Father?" asked Owen fearfully.

His father sighed. "I'm afraid he can. He's tricked me. I can't pay the money by May Day—it's the day after tomorrow."

Owen tried to hide his tears as he went to bed. He considered himself too old to cry, so it must be that the rain blew in on his pillow that night.

The next day Mr. O'Flaherty went, without much hope, to argue with Burke.

Owen looked so woebegone that his mother said, "You and the girls see if you can catch some fish for dinner. I'll give you some bread to eat by the lake."

So the children took the lunch, and Owen took his fiddle, and they headed across the field.

Owen's heart sank when he saw Burke fishing in their favorite place. But the boy politely called an old Irish greeting, "Good morning, Mr. Burke. May the sun shine warm upon your face."

Burke growled, "Get away with your noise. You'll scare the fish. Be off with you!"

The O'Flaherty children backed away.

Owen looked at his sisters' sad faces. Then he said,
"We can prop our poles against a rock and sit some-
where else."

Meg asked, "Will you put the worm on my hook,
Owen? I don't like worms."

So Owen did. Then he and the girls went up under
the fairy thorn. Owen played his fiddle.

Mary and Meg listened, entranced. It was a beautiful tune with the lilts and slurs of the old-time music. It was so lovely that Owen didn't want it to end. He played it three times over.

"Are you wanting something?" asked an oddly musical voice as Owen finished.

The children looked around and saw a man in shabby clothes standing by Burke.

"I'm wanting to be alone," Burke said sharply.

"Oh," said the stranger, "I thought perhaps you'd share your lunch with a poor old man."

"No," Burke said. "I have no lunch to share. That's a package of . . . of worms . . . for bait."

"Worms?" repeated the stranger. "If you say so."

"Hello," called Owen. "Will you share our lunch? We'd be honored, I'm sure."

"I will indeed," said the stranger, and he leaped up the bank and doffed his hat with a bow. The little girls giggled.

Owen opened the package of lunch, saying, "It's not much, sir, but you're welcome to it." Then he stared. Not only was there bread and butter, but cheese and fruit and soda bread with raisins.

"How entirely fortunate that Mother packed such a grand lunch!" Owen thought to himself as he passed it around.

"Help yourself, Mr.—ah—"

"Ah, Finn. Just call me Mr. Finn," said their guest with a smile. "Tell me, who taught you the fiddle tune you played a moment ago?"

"No one taught me exactly, Mr. Finn. I heard my grandfather play it many times. When he gave me his fiddle, he promised to teach me his special tune. But he never did. I've thought and thought about that tune until finally I could hear it in my head. Once I hear it in my head, my fingers can find the tune on the strings."

Mr. Finn nodded. "'Tis a fine tune. If you're as good at fishing as you are at fiddling, you should have a good catch."

Owen ran down the bank to see. There was a fat trout on each line! He scrambled back up the bank, shouting, "Mr. Finn! You've brought us luck!"

Before Mr. Finn could reply he was interrupted by Burke who stormed up, shaking his fist.

"You good-for-nothing O'Flahertys! You stole my lunch and left me worms."

"What?" said Owen.

"Why, Mr. Burke," said Mr. Finn, "you told me yourself that you had no lunch, only worms for bait."

Burke, red in the face, broke a switch from the fairy thorn and struck at the children.

"Away with you! I'll have no playing on my property!"

The little girls began to cry. Owen stood his ground. "That's a fairy thorn," he said. "It's bad luck to break it."

"I make my own luck," Burke declared. "Let the fairies look out for themselves." And he stalked away.

Owen had never felt so helpless and miserable.

Mr. Finn murmured, "Long as day is, night comes."

The eve of May Day was a sad one indeed for the O'Flahertys. On other years the children had scampered around the farm, setting charms, for May Eve is the fairies' night to make mischief.

Even those people who claim not to believe in fairies usually take care on May Eve. They put a horseshoe under the churn or tie a nail to the cow's tail or put a pat of butter on the gatepost.

Tonight Owen and Meg and Mary did these things in silence, kissed their parents, and went to bed early.

Owen couldn't sleep. He heard his father groan. "May Eve . . . and the last night we shall spend in our own home. What can we do? What can we do?"

His mother sighed. "Grandfather once hinted that he could summon the fairies for help. If only we knew how."

Owen sat up in bed. He thought, "If Grandfather could summon the fairies, maybe I could myself. But how? Call to them? No, if it were that simple everyone could do it. Maybe . . . maybe by playing Grandfather's special tune! Maybe that's what made it special."

Wide-eyed in the dark, Owen made his plan.

The fire was dead on the hearth and the things of the night were abroad when Owen picked up his fiddle and tiptoed outside.

It was dark. Clouds like tattered ghosts chased by the wind fled across the sky. Shadows crouched under bushes like demons waiting to leap.

Owen shivered but moved bravely toward the fairy thorn. Once under its sheltering branches he took a deep breath, put the fiddle under his chin, and began to play his grandfather's special tune.

He played it once, then he waited hopefully—and fearfully—for fairies to appear. The moon hid its face behind a cloud, but nothing else happened.

Owen played the tune a second time. Nothing. He wiped his sweaty hands and played the tune a third time.

" 'Tis a fine tune," said a voice behind him.

Owen whirled around, his heart in his throat. But it was only old Mr. Finn.

"Oh," said Owen, "it's you, Mr. Finn."

"And who was it you were expecting?"

So Owen told his hope that the special tune would summon fairies to help him save the O'Flaherty farm and his fiddle from Mr. Burke.

"But nothing happened," Owen finished sadly. "I guess there are no fairies in Ireland anymore."

Mr. Finn threw back his head and laughed. And as he laughed, a strange thing happened. He grew taller and younger. His old coat fell away, revealing a suit of silver armor that clung like salmon scales to his slender body.

"You call me Mr. Finn. Now can you guess my real name?"

"Are you ... are you Fin ... Finvarra, the King of the Fairies?"

"I am indeed!" cried Finvarra. "And I came in answer to your special tune, just as I did before. But only on May Eve can I enter the mortal world dressed like a king. That tune is called 'The King of the Fairies' and I myself taught it to your grandfather when he did me a good turn years ago. Now, Owen O'Flaherty, come with me to my home in the Hill of Knockma!"

Finvarra turned to the fairy thorn. Suddenly a door opened where no door had been. Finvarra led the way into a long tunnel lighted by golden apples hanging on silver chains. Owen followed.

The tunnel opened into a large chamber. Owen's eyes grew big with wonder. The ceiling was soft with yellow feathers. The walls sparkled with precious gems. Even more amazing were the creatures there.

On one side were Finvarra's fairy host dressed in crimson cloaks and silver plumes. They were saddling their horses with ruby studded silver trappings.

On the other side were the leprechauns, who were very small indeed. These fairies were not clothed so splendidly, but each one played with a heap of gold coins, stacking them high or tumbling them about.

"Now, Owen," said Finvarra, "because you gave me bread, I will give you jewels, as many as you need to keep Burke from taking your farm."

"Oh," cried Owen, "but—but Burke won't accept jewels I'm thinking. He will claim they are not real or else stolen."

"True for you," Finvarra agreed. Then the same thought struck both of them. They turned to look at the leprechauns' gold.

Finvarra said courteously to the oldest of the little men, "Sir, could you spare some gold for my friend Owen O'Flaherty?"

The leprechaun king said, "Let him prove to us that he is deserving and he shall have the gold."

"What test do you suggest?" asked Finvarra.

"Just that he play a tune on his fiddle," said the leprechaun king. "Just that."

There was much laughter among the leprechauns and they gathered around with mischievous smiles.

Finvarra frowned, but he said to Owen, "You can win the gold. Just play a tune and don't stop, whatever happens."

Owen felt a cold chill. He looked around him. The leprechauns seemed friendly, 'twas true, but they were fairy folk and he did not belong in their land.

"You can win," came Finvarra's voice again.

Owen lifted his fiddle and began to play. There was stillness in the fairy chamber as the notes rose, sweet and true and strong.

Gradually the boy's fiddle felt so strange and heavy on his arm that he glanced down—and found himself looking into the eyes of a wild pig! His left hand grasped the beast's hind leg and its sharp tusks were at his shoulder. But it still sounded like his fiddle. He glanced wildly at Finvarra, who stared steadily back. Owen clenched his teeth and played on.

Then his bow became a wriggling black snake that lifted its evil head and lunged at him. Owen did not flinch. He closed his eyes, the better to ignore the frightening thing. Although his heart pounded, he played on.

But even with his eyes shut, Owen knew when his fiddle burst into flame. He heard the crackling of the wood, smelled the smoke, and felt the fire on his hands and face.

"It's only fairy fire," he told himself. But oh! it burned! Family . . . farm . . . fiddle . . . Finvarra. . . .

He clung to these thoughts amidst the smoke and pain and music. Then the pain drifted away with the smoke, and Owen opened his eyes to Finvarra's proud smile. He had won!

The fairy fiddlers were playing with him now, and the dancers whirled gaily. The leprechaun king stood on tiptoe and stuffed a bulging purse filled with gold into Owen's pocket.

Joyfully Owen fiddled on until a bell began to ring. Everyone stopped to listen, counting the chimes. Then "Midnight!" they cheered and ran for their horses.

Finvarra mounted his horse, jet black as a beetle's back. He seized Owen's arm and swung him up behind him. The ceiling cracked asunder and out of the Hill of Knockma rushed the fairies.

They swept up into the black sky and scattered over the countryside, helter-skelter, intent on mischief.

Woe to the man who had failed to put out food or drink for the fairies that night! Woe to the man who had disturbed the white hawthorn tree or the fairy forts!

"Woe to Mr. Burke!" shouted Finvarra as they swooped toward his silent house.

Foolish Burke had not put primroses across the doorway to protect his barn, so the fairies milked all his cows. He had not put a pat of butter on the gatepost for them, so they took all the butter.

More than that, the fairies poured sand in the sugar bowl and water in the flour bin.

Four fairies tilted Burke's bed and spilled him out on the floor. Thump! He awoke. The fairies were invisible to him so he thought he had merely fallen out of bed. He tried to get back in, but the fairies bounced the bed up and down. A pillow burst and feathers fell like snow.

"What a frightful dream I'm having," Burke whimpered. He gave a howl as one of the fairies dropped a stool on his bare toes.

Then Burke heard a knock on the door. It was Owen, who said, "I've come with the money."

"I'll teach you to play tricks on me!" Burke shouted. He grabbed the switch he had broken from the fairy thorn and aimed a blow at Owen.

Finvarra, standing unseen by Burke, commanded, " hi knop sᴄıᴄꞣeᴄꞑ!"

The thorn switch twisted in Burke's hand and began to beat the old man himself.

"Ow!" Burke howled. He grasped the stick, thinking he could break it. The stick shook him up and down until his eyes bulged and his teeth rattled.

Burke let go and picked up his heavy cane. Crack!
He hit the fairy thorn switch and it broke in two and
fell to the floor.

Burke, red faced and furious, turned on Owen,
but the boy cried, " hɪ knop stɪckety!"

The two pieces of the fairy thorn rapped like
drumsticks on Burke's bald head!

It was too much. "Stop! You win!" Burke yelled.

"ḣı sṫop sṫıckeṫy," ordered Finvarra, and the fairy thorn was still.

With a happy heart, Owen counted out the money. Then with his hand on the door he called, "Good night, Mr. Burke. May the wind be always at your back."

Burke did not answer, he just wiped his nose on his sleeve.

Owen laughed with Finvarra and skipped home, the rest of the gold jingling in his pocket. And the O'Flahertys from that grand day to this have been friends of the fairies.

The King of the Fairies

The story of *The Fairy Thorn* was inspired by the chance remark of a friend to Gerry and George Armstrong. She said, "Throughout Ireland you'll notice the white hawthorn standing alone in a field. The farmers never touch it. We call it the May Tree because it blooms around the first of May." This bit of information plus a fascination with Celtic folklore led the Armstrongs to Ireland, to County Galway and the Hill of Knockma, the setting of this tale. The legend of Finvarra and the customs associated with May Day are taken from Irish tradition.

Two other beautiful picture books by the Armstrongs, *The Magic Bagpipe* and *The Boat on the Hill*, also grew out of firsthand experiences on visits, one to Scotland and the other to Cornwall.

Gerry Armstrong, who has written this trilogy of tales about the British Isles, is Irish on her father's side of her family. The Breens came from County Clare. George Armstrong is of Scots-English descent, and this may explain his love of the bagpipe, which he has played since he was eleven. His illustrations and maps appear in textbooks and encyclopedias from many publishers. He specializes in history and folklore.

The Armstrongs and their daughters, Becky and Jenny, are nationally known in folk-music circles. They have made two albums of records of Anglo-American traditional songs and have given radio and television concerts both here and abroad. Their home is in Wilmette, Illinois.